Roxanne

W9-AAE-052

Grumpy Cat
This Book Stinks!

By **Christy Webster**

Illustrated by **Patrick Spaziante**

Random House 🏠 New York

Copyright © 2019 by Grumpy Cat Limited. All rights reserved. Published in the United States by Random House Children's Books, a division of Penguin Random House LLC, 1745 Broadway, New York, NY 10019, and in Canada by Penguin Random House Canada Limited, Toronto. Grumpy Cat Images Copyright and "Grumpy Cat"® Trademark are the exclusive property of Grumpy Cat Limited, Ohio, USA.

grumpycats.com
rhcbooks.com
ISBN 978-1-9848-5129-1
MANUFACTURED IN CHINA
10 9 8 7 6 5 4 3 2 1

Grumpy Cat and Pokey are sister and brother.
Pokey likes everything. Grumpy just wants to be left alone.
  "Don't you love the smell of fresh flowers?" Pokey asked
Grumpy one day.

  "No," Grumpy Cat replied, and jumped up
on the porch.

Pokey followed Grumpy to the front porch. The humans had left behind two cups of hot chocolate.

"Grumpy Cat, that hot chocolate smells sooooo sweet!" Pokey said.

"Too sweet," Grumpy Cat said, and went inside.

Pokey followed Grumpy Cat into the living room. "Oh, Grumpy Cat!" Pokey cried. "Those shiny oranges smell so fresh!"

"I'll leave you to enjoy them,"
Grumpy Cat said, and ran upstairs.

Pokey followed Grumpy Cat into the bedroom.
"These things smell wonderful!" Pokey said.
"The humans really know how to live, don't they?"

"No," Grumpy Cat said, and ducked into the bathroom.

Pokey followed Grumpy Cat into the bathroom.

"Look, Grumpy Cat!" Pokey said. "A nice, soapy bath!"

"I don't think so," Grumpy Cat said,
and went back downstairs.

Pokey followed Grumpy Cat down to the basement. "What luck!" Pokey said. "Clean laundry! Now *this* is my favorite smell."

While Pokey was playing in the basket,
Grumpy Cat slipped out to the backyard.

Pokey followed Grumpy Cat outside.
"There's nothing like the smell of
suntan lotion on a sunny day!"
Pokey said.

"Nothing worse," Grumpy Cat replied,
and slinked off into the garden.

Pokey followed Grumpy Cat into the vegetable garden. "Why do you keep leaving?" Pokey asked. "Don't you love all these wonderful smells?"

"No," Grumpy Cat said,
and went back inside.

Pokey followed Grumpy Cat into the kitchen.
"Oh, I know!" Pokey said. "You wanted to get to the kitchen
to smell this freshly baked bread!"

Grumpy Cat just kept walking.

Pokey followed Grumpy Cat into the pantry.
Grumpy Cat found a nice place to sit among the onions.
"Grumpy Cat, this pantry stinks of onions!"
Pokey exclaimed. "I can't stay in here." Pokey left.
Grumpy Cat was finally alone.

"I like this smell."